This book belongs to...

Places I must see..!?
Eiffel Tower - called
Tour Eiffel.
Louvre Museum - is
called Musée du Louvre
Palace of Versailles - is called
Château de Versailles
Notre Dame - is called
Cathédrale Notre Dame de Paris

Mr Chicken
goes to Paris

(Monsieur Poulet va à Paris)

Leigh HOBBS

ALLEN & UNWIN

For Julia Murray

First published in 2009

Allen & Unwin
83 Alexander St
Crows Nest NSW 2065
Australia
Phone: (61 2) 8425 0100
Fax: (61 2) 9906 2218
Email: info@allenandunwin.com
Web: www.allenandunwin.com

National Library of Australia
Cataloguing-in-Publication entry:

Hobbs, Leigh.

Mr Chicken goes to Paris / Leigh Hobbs.

ISBN: 978 1 74175 769 9 (hbk.)

For children.

Chickens—Juvenile fiction.
Paris (France)—Juvenile fiction.

A823.3

Cover design by Leigh Hobbs and Sandra Nobes
Text design by Sandra Nobes
Set in Cochin by Sandra Nobes
Colour reproduction by Splitting Image, Clayton, Victoria
Printed in China by 1010 Printing International Limited

1 3 5 7 9 10 8 6 4 2

www.leighhobbs.com

Thanks to Sandra Nobes, Sheralyn Bavinton, Ric Benson and Elise Jones for their invaluable assistance.
And of course Erica Wagner, without whom this book …

Mr Chicken loved to travel.
His French friend Yvette had invited him to visit,
so he studied his maps, grabbed his camera
and caught a taxi to the airport.

Mr Chicken flew to France.
Paris, to be exact …

... economy.

As the clouds parted, Mr Chicken
was thrilled to see Paris way down below.
'Fasten your seat-belt please, sir,' said the air hostess.
'We are about to land.'

When he arrived, Yvette was there to greet him.
'Bonjour, Monsieur Poulet. Welcome to Paris.'
'Bonjour, Yvette!' said Mr Chicken. 'How wonderful to see you!'

Mr Chicken was tired after his long flight, but rest was out of the question.
He was keen to see the sights, so Yvette bought a museum pass
and travel card for two.

After years of looking at pictures in books,
Mr Chicken could hardly believe he was really in Paris.

On the way to the Arc de Triomphe,
he politely asked someone to take his photo.
'Of course, monsieur,' came the reply.
'Merci, madame,' said Mr Chicken.

On top of the Arc de Triomphe
he studied his list of helpful
French phrases and cried, 'Magnifique!'

Mr Chicken took lots of photos for his album
before he and Yvette hopped back on the bus.
It was time to see some art
at the Musée du Louvre.

After five minutes, Mr Chicken was exhausted.
He was thinking of sitting down and having a cake when
Yvette said, 'Look, the Mona Lisa!'

'It's lovely,' said Mr Chicken, licking his lips.
He took a photo, and bought a postcard. Best of all,
he found a special Mona Lisa tea-towel for his kitchen back at home.

Soon after, there was a strange
rumbling in Mr Chicken's tummy.
'Er, pardon me,' he said.
'Maybe we should have lunch?'
said Yvette.
'Oh, yes please, er, oui! Oui!' said
Mr Chicken, practising his French.

'Superbe!' he said, after
enjoying two frog-leg soufflés
on board the tourist boat.

To help him blend in
and feel French,
Yvette took Mr Chicken
for a ride on the Métro.

All went well until
he got lost.

To make matters worse,
he forgot his French.
So no one understood
when he asked for help.

What a relief it was when he heard a familiar voice.
'Monsieur Poulet! *This* way to the Eiffel Tower.'
It was Yvette.

The queue was long and Mr Chicken was far too excited to wait for the lift.

So he made his own way to the top, where he and Yvette admired the view.

Back on the streets of Paris, Yvette waited patiently while Mr Chicken had his portrait painted.

He blushed when she said, 'It looks just like you.'

There was so much to do and see and eat in Paris
that Mr Chicken nearly overheated.
Just in time, he found a place to cool down.

'I think we need to go somewhere quiet,' said Yvette.

'This,' Yvette whispered,
'is the most famous church
in all of France.'

The inside of Notre Dame
was certainly beautiful,
but Mr Chicken had
his heart set on the
roof-top tour.

The roof-top tour was thrilling.
What's more, Mr Chicken found a
special place to play in the bell tower.

Next was a trip to the
Palace of Versailles in a taxi
with a sunroof.

'Queen Marie Antoinette lived here,' said Yvette.

Mr Chicken was impressed. In fact, he thought he might like to move in.

'Come,' said Yvette. 'Let's look inside.'

The rooms were huge, and so alas was Mr Chicken's waistline.
'I might have to go on a diet,' he thought in the Hall of Mirrors,
catching a glimpse of a great big bottom.

At dinnertime, however, the diet was forgotten.

'It all looks delicious,' said Mr Chicken. 'I'll have everything on the menu.'

A perfect day was nearly over.

And so was Mr Chicken's visit.

'Au revoir, Monsieur Poulet,' said Yvette, at the airport.

'Au revoir, Yvette,' said a tearful Mr Chicken.

But right at the last minute, there was a great big problem. While his luggage could fit on the plane, poor Mr Chicken could not.

Luckily, clever Yvette came to the rescue with a splendid idea.

So Mr Chicken, and his souvenirs,
could fly home after all … first class.

What a wonderful day it had been!

Tuesday.
Dear Yvette
Thank you for
a wonderful
day. (merci!)
I shall send
you some
photographs
very soon.
Best wishes from
your friend
monsieur Poulet.

To, Yvette.
Paris
FRANCE.